Snow White
and
The Seven
Cannibals

LAURA HAWKS

ISBN: 0-9976594-3-2
ISBN-13: 978-0-9976594-3-6

AUTHOR'S NOTE

This is darker version of Snow White where the Dwarfs are not sweet and endearing but instead are sadistic and cruel. This story is a work of fiction. Any resemblance to actual persons, living or dead, event or locals is coincidental. This story is loosely based off Grimm's Fairytales published in 1812.

DEDICATION

For my mother. Always and forever she will be in my
heart. I miss her terribly.
Thanks also to my fans, and friends who have kept me
going when I just wanted to give up.
For the dreamer in all of us.. this is dedicated to you, the
reader.

Prologue

The sun shone brightly, yet she wouldn't know it as she walked the deeply shaded forest path. The tall, dark trees intertwined their branches to others as if they were holding hands in some romantic gesture. It didn't matter to her. She was young, free, and enjoying the ability to explore the world around her. Like most ten year olds, she didn't have much of a care of the things that go bump in the night.

She skipped down the sodden path, curious and excited to know where it would lead, but she stopped when she heard a whimper followed by a deep roar. The latter was so loud it scattered birds into the air and she could hear the fluttering beat of their wings as they took flight in rapid haste.

Snow White stopped, turning around slowly, trying to determine from which direction such a pitiful cry had emanated. As a youth, she wasn't scared of the roar, only as to what it might pertain. She hated to have anyone or anything hurt, and if she could help, she was going to. After a few moments, she figured that the sound came from the direction she was originally headed and continued on the dirt path. It had rained recently, so the ground was almost spongy with the dirt mixed with leaves and small plants. The mud still covered her shoes and ankles, as well as the hem of her light blue dress. Still, she didn't care. She wanted to find the animal that might be in pain. If she could give it aid, she would.

The woods became quiet again, still. Even the birds seemed to have been silenced by the cry from whatever animal bellowed. The only sounds were her feet padding against the ground and her breathing. She worried she would be too late to assist the creature, especially since she wasn't sure where it was. It must have sensed someone coming to aid it, for moments later she could hear a slight whimpering and let the sound lead her towards it.

Soon other sounds, those of men's indistinguishable talking, became noticeable. Something warned her to be cautious as she approached, ducking down behind some bushes to watch what was going on in the clearing just ahead. Anger at what she was witnessing made her want to storm in and make them stop, but she knew she couldn't win against seven of them.

The men were small and reminded her of those garden gnomes her mother loved and had scattered about the palace gardens. Only these men weren't wearing pointy hats. They were wearing caps like one would find on a peddler or on men who lived near the ocean. It was their taunting of the captured animal that infuriated her. She had to do something, and yet she knew she was outmanned and outnumbered. So, she continued to hide and await her chance to set the animal free.

The animal wasn't like anything Snow had ever seen in her life, outside of books she had been given in her school studies. Yet, it was distinctive enough she knew immediately what it was. A gorgeous male lion was tied, his tawny fur matted and covered in mud, dirt, and blood. His full mane around his face must be beautiful when clean, but it looked dingy as it clung to his neck. He tried to lunge at the gnomes when they approached, but they had him too secure to get very far without injuring himself further with the effort.

The ropes were wrapped around his paws, his mid-section, and his neck. The men were taunting him with sticks and spears, but nothing that would kill him immediately. It was as if they enjoyed torturing their captive beast. One threw rocks at him as they taunted him. The lion roared again, then turned his amber eyes towards her. He stared right at her, as if he knew she was there crouching low in the bushes, watching.

Snow knew she had to do something, but she wasn't sure what. She was only a kid; she didn't know how to fight or anything. A bell sounded in the distance and she couldn't believe her luck as the seven men turned and sauntered away, leaving the lion alone for a few moments. Snow didn't waste time; she ran out from her hiding place and looked for a way to get the lion free. She searched for some way to loosen the ropes before she realized she was having no success and needed to do something else before the men returned.

The lion watched her, remaining silent but shaking his head towards the way the men had left. She turned in fear they might be returning when she saw the axe against a nearby tree. She ran to retrieve it. One good swing and maybe she could cut through the cord to free him. However, she found it much heavier than she anticipated when she went to pick it up. She virtually dragged it back to the lion, but she knew she had to do this in order to save him. The creature seemed to understand she was there to free him, so remained silent and still. Snow looked for a place to cut the rope without being near the lion itself. She dreaded the idea she might swing, miss, and hit him by accident. Gathering up every bit of strength she had, she lifted the axe over her head and swung down. She missed the rope completely. She didn't give it a second thought, but lifted it again, this time hitting the hemp cord. It took her five additional swings to cut through. Once one end of the rope was severed, the rest was easily maneuvered to free him. She moved to pull the cord from around his neck and used the loose end to untangle it from his mid-section. The lion stepped out of the enclosures to his legs and limped towards freedom. Only when he reached the line of trees did the king of the jungle turn and give her a look, bowing his head slightly in gratitude and thanks.

It was then she heard the men coming back and ran back to the area she had emerged from. The men immediately noticed their captive prey gone and they saw the light blue of her dress as it disappeared into the bushes. They quickly gave chase, waving sticks, axes, and spears in the air. She ran, her breath becoming labored, her legs getting tired. The darkness of the forest seemed to close in on her, suffocating her. She turned to see how far behind they were and tripped, falling onto her knees as she hit the ground. Her ear now against the dirt, she could hear their heavy footsteps, and when she turned to look again they were right on top of her. She screamed.

The room filled with her screams and she felt herself being shaken.

"Shh. It's okay, Snow. It's only a dream. It's only a dream. You're safe." Her mother's voice pierced the cobwebs of sleep away as well as the lingering nightmare Snow had been having the past month. She clung to her mother as tightly as her nightgown was clinging to her with her sweat.

"Did she have that nightmare again?" her father asked from the doorway of her room.

Her mother nodded. "Yes. I believe so."

Snow nodded, unable to say anything as tears ran down her face and a lump of emotion stuck in her throat.

The king moved to Snow's bed and knelt beside her, holding out a stuffed lion toy. "I thought maybe this lion will keep you safe. Since you saved his life, he kind of owes you and will guard you."

Snow wiped her eyes and reached for the toy her father had given her, clutching it tightly. The amber eyes of the tawny lion in her dreams had stuck with her each day and the toy had the same coloring. She had a feeling he had it specially made for her and she was extremely grateful for his generous thoughtfulness.

Chapter One

Once a upon a time, a beautiful woman with skin as white as snow and hair as black as night was determined to explore the forbidden forest that lay just beyond the palace window. How many days had she sat at the window wishing she could go through it? As she sat, she held a slightly worn stuffed lion on her lap. She could remember the day she got the toy from her father to help keep the nightmares away. It worked because her sleep had been uninterrupted since, but she still had the desire to venture out and explore the world beyond the gates for herself.

For as long as Snow White remembered she awoke to the sight of the lush land beyond her home. Every night, the harmonious sounds of nearby creatures that inhabited the area, as well as the rustling leaves, lulled and soothed her to sleep. For years she'd envisioned what the emerald jungle was like. However, she never had the opportunity to romp and play in the beckoning woods because her parents forbade her venturing outside the safety of the palace walls. Were they fearful her nightmare would become reality? They never mentioned it, instead giving her a myriad of other excuses as to why she couldn't investigate the wooded area.

"Princesses don't play in such common places. Princesses don't get dirty. Princesses don't traipse where it's dangerous." How many times had those words been admonished to her? She'd heard them over and over so often that they rang in her head every moment she thought about sneaking out and exploring. Not in years had she actually attempted to venture beyond the gates of the castle that encompassed her entire life and sometimes made her feel like a prisoner. She'd never been able to venture beyond the gates of the palace and was kept ignorant of what lay beyond. There were times she wondered if her childhood nightmare might be real and that was why she had been prohibited to travel away from her home, and she was fearful at the thought. To this day, ten years later, she still could remember the dark dream and feel the frightening emotions it wrought within her. She could also remember the feeling of power and need from the lion being tortured by the creatures who had captured him. She'd been willing to do anything to set such a proud beast free. She'd have done the same in reality, should the need ever arise, but this was not an area that had lions or any other dangerous creatures, at least as far as she was aware.

Today, she knew she was to meet another suitor. She had already met several over the past few months, but none appealed to her. Regardless, she knew she was running out of time to travel into the forest and investigate. She wasn't sure what she was looking for, she was just sure she would know it when she saw it. She would feel it in her heart and soul when she met the right man for her. As silly as it sounded, she wanted him to have the heart of a lion—brave, strong, loyal, and affectionate. So far, those she met were anything but. Usually mousy, or weak, or a little too dandyish for her taste. And some were downright scary, giving her cause for some concern when they were alone, enough to know she didn't want to live out her life with such a man.

As Snow sat peering out the window upon the dense green landscape, she firmly decided she was going to explore the woods. Something called to her and she could no longer ignore the siren's vociferation the forest emitted. Time was running out, she could feel it as if it were a tangible presence. It made her flush with a feeling she'd never encountered before. Thoughts of a strong man caressing her skin, kissing her lips, and her body which made her quake in parts she never knew about excited her, yet scared her. She had a meeting to meet another suitor later that day and for some reason, she had the feeling this might be the one, even though she couldn't comprehend why.

She realized if she snuck out of the palace, she could traverse there and back before anyone even noticed she was missing. Considering she hadn't tried to escape in years, she was sure this time she'd be successful. Although, she knew she had to hurry.

Dressing quickly, she headed downstairs and slipped outside. Pulling the dark cloak tight about her slender form, Snow White was sure she was safe from being discovered. Suddenly however, she found her path blocked by a hulking shadow. Her eyes followed up the darkened visage to realize that her way was prevented by one of the palace guards.

Startled, the princess gasped, taking a step back until she recognized Reed, her personal bodyguard who'd been with her for most of her life. The imposing yet perceptive royal dragoon had seen her attempt to depart the safety of the palace garden and intercepted her escape.

Reed couldn't believe in the last hour before meeting another suitor she'd undertake flight beyond the palace walls. How many attempts had he prevented when she was but a child? Then the nightmares came, and her inquisitiveness had dwindled and stopped. He was aware there was still a minute part of her that dreamed of delving into the unknown only glimpsed from her bedroom window, but he thought she'd outgrown such fruitless endeavors. Although he stood with arms crossed as his dark eyes glared at the petite woman before him, he could never be truly angry with her; he cared about her too much to be fully upset with her. In truth, he loved her as much as the whole palace and village did. She was kind, beautiful, and caring, traits that assured her place among her people. He knew the dangers that lay beyond the walls of the castle, but like the other servants of the realm, was forbidden to speak of it, especially to the young princess.

Reed watched her grow from an inquisitive child who tried to run into the woods almost daily until the nightmares came, through her teen years where her kindness began to blossom even though she held onto the vestiges of youth with her stuffed lion, and then into the gorgeous woman whose generous, sweet spirit was unrivaled in the realm. When he saw her cloaked figure and quickly realized what she was about to attempt, something he'd not seen from her in years, he employed the shortcut used during her slightly wayward youth to prevent her success and block her escape. He knew he didn't have to say anything beyond the glare and stance, for he had cautioned her many times in her youthful past.

Snow White, however, wasn't about to be prevented from her goal this time. For the past twenty years, she'd followed all the instructions given to her without question. Almost every day for the past couple of months suitors came to her kingdom, plying for her hand in marriage. She knew one day she would accept a suitor and then be forced to leave without ever knowing what lay beyond the palace window of her room. She felt compelled to explore, felt this was her last chance, her final opportunity to do so. If she could convince Reed maybe, just maybe he'd allow her to investigate the world beyond the walls of her home. Lifting her chin in regal defiance, she peered at the palace guard.

"Either step aside or come with me, but I *am* going to explore the woods today."

"Princess!" Reed admonished, despite seeing a determination he rarely saw in her. Even when she made attempts as a youth she would meekly return to her room, albeit sometimes contritely and occasionally angry. "You're aware that it's dangerous as well as forbidden. After all these years, why now are you trying to break your father's rules?"

"I'm princess of the realm, am I not? Why is it forbidden for me to roam the land that I will rule with my future husband? Should I not get to know those that lay yonder, beyond the walls of my home? Shouldn't I see with my own eyes that which needs to be governed, so as to be a better, more efficient ruler?" Snow White saw that she was breaking through his reserve with her words. Relaxing her stance a bit more, she moved closer to him and touched his arm lightly. "Please, Reed. I won't have many more chances. Don't take this opportunity from me. Come with me and let me explore. No one will know and if anyone finds out, I'll take full responsibility for my own actions. Please." She paused a moment, trying to find a way to sway him. "You can protect me. I know it." She'd avoided the one thing that would force him. She didn't want to be overbearing by commanding him, though if discovered, she'd tell her parents he'd no choice in the matter because she gave him an order and he had to obey her bidding.

The pleading look in her eyes, her gentle voice, and her soft touch undid him. Reed could refuse her nothing for he was putty in her hands. He wouldn't let her go alone. Maybe if she saw just a touch of the woods at the edge of the forest she might rest more easily in her desire to investigate the unknown land.

"A short excursion? And we stay near the palace?"

She nodded eagerly. Her hope turned to anticipation with his words allowing her to enter the darkened world which enticed her with its intricately hidden secrets. "Yes. A brief interlude to explore."

He lowered his arms and drew his sword, keeping it lowered but at the ready for whatever danger might come, and yet he hoped they would encounter none of the evil that lived freely within the depths of the forest.

"After you, Princess Snow." He bowed slightly as she passed him and entered the world beyond her private domain through the small unmanned gate within the stone wall.

Chapter Two

Prince Donnigan rode steadily on his solid black Friesian mare as he approached the scrolling wrought-iron castle gates. He was scheduled to meet Princess Snow White, who, to date, had turned down every suitor she'd seen. Her beauty was renowned. Her wisdom and intelligence were acclaimed. Her kindness was legendary. The princess would be the perfect wife to be at his side and rule the lands that would be joined with their marriage, should she agree to be his spouse. He had even heard she liked lions, which was an added bonus as he liked them also.

Donnigan hadn't thought about taking a wife, but his parents had been asking for an heir of late and he didn't want to disappoint them if he could avoid it. Granted, he tried over the past several years, but all for naught. The princesses he had met were admittedly beautiful, at least on the outside, but some were power hungry while others were interested in his finances. Some were skittish and hid behind their mother's skirts. He didn't want a woman like that. He wanted one who could stand on her own, do what was right, even if it was against everyone else's ideas, and one who would be a fitting complement to him.

He was attractive, with shoulder-length, sandy-blonde hair and amber eyes. His shoulders were broad, leading down to a narrow waist in that perfect V men had. He had made a name for himself over the last decade, proving himself worthy to take his father's place when the time was right. Known for his altruistic tendencies and fighting skills, he represented the finest the Panthera Kingdom had to offer. He could and would prove to any woman who was his equal that he would make her a wonderful partner in life. He had high hopes and a good feeling Princess Snow would be the one who finally met his approval, and he hoped he would meet hers. Was it so wrong to want a woman who embodied most of the qualities he was looking for, someone who would complement him and offer him advice? To be his confidant and his heart? To accept him and all his secrets, and still love him with all of her heart? His father found a woman like that. Donnigan wanted no less for himself, and he hoped Princess Snow White might be the answer to his dreams.

Having finally approached the steps leading to the palace, he dismounted his steed. Greeted by the doorman, Prince Donnigan was led to the receiving hall and asked to wait. The prince expected this, as the others liked to use this time to observe him surreptitiously. He tugged on his waistcoat and moved around the receiving room admiring the paintings, especially those of the royal family, which included the princess of the realm. He had gotten so lost in the portraits he hadn't realized how much time he had been there until he noticed the shadows shifting within the room. A couple of hours had passed and he was beginning to get irritated at being made to bide his time for so long. Surely they would've had plenty of time by now to observe him? He couldn't have disappointed them already, without having even exchanged words. He didn't fully expect that she'd refuse to even give him a chance by not even arriving to meet him. Furious at his own imagination as to the delay, he was about to demand an audience and inquire about the delay when King Nicholas entered the room surrounded by palace guards and weeping maids. Prince Donnigan's fury instantly abated as he wondered what tragedy precipitated such a display.

King Nicholas appeared saddened and deflated, as if from a great loss. Donnigan waited for the elder male to speak, standing proudly before the noble ruler.

"My sincerest apologies for keeping you waiting, Prince Donnigan. I know you've traveled quite a way to vie for the privilege of meeting my daughter and maybe obtain her hand in marriage, but an unexpected event has occurred. I've just recently been informed of the situation. It appears my strong-willed daughter has succeeded in sneaking out into the woods beyond our walls. Most likely to explore, despite being told it was forbidden and dangerous. It's, sadly, something she'd always been fascinated with. I assume she felt the need even more so as of late, knowing she'd leave for whichever husband's kingdom she chooses to spend her life with." King Nicholas paused for a moment and lowered his head in defeat. "She doesn't know what the forest contains, or the evil ones that roam freely. We've been unable to prevent the terrorization of our lands that have existed for decades, nor have we been able to rid ourselves of the problem."

Prince Donnigan's eyes blazed with anger. How could the king hide such things from such a seemingly intelligent woman as his own daughter? The prince was all too aware of the issues King Nicholas' people endured. Since Donnigan himself was special, he was sure he could aide in ending the problem. Yet to not disclose all the dangers hiding in the forest beyond the palace gates to his grown daughter was incomprehensible.

Nicholas added softly, "Snow White is very stubborn, and despite repeated warnings has attempted several times to sneak into the woods. She'd always been prevented in the past. This time, her personal bodyguard allowed her to succeed by taking her into the dark realm himself!"

Prince Donnigan growled. "Her bodyguard *took* her into the woods? Is he a fool or does he not care for the safety of the heir to your kingdom? Why was the situation never fully explained to her? You yourself have said she's intelligent. I've heard of her wisdom and sagacity in lands as far as my own realm. Surely, had you spent time to explain the circumstances, she'd have been more amenable to following your instructions of not venturing into such a dangerous area in order to satisfy her own curiosity."

The king's head snapped up. "She'd never disobeyed my wishes before."

"You should've been honest with her instead of trying to just order her about. You should've treated her like the adult and future ruler she's to be, rather than a child who is kept in the dark of the horrors the world contains."

Prince Donnigan spun on his heel and headed out of the room, calling back, "When I find her and return her safely to this castle, you *will* always be honest with her."

The king sat down heavily on his throne as hope washed through him for the first time in the past few hours. "You bring her back safely, I'll give you anything you desire."

Prince Donnigan stopped at the doorway and looked back over his shoulder. "I'll take you up on that, but you might not like my fees as much as you think." With that last utterance, Donnigan headed outside, climbed on his horse, and headed into the wooded land alone to find the wayward princess.

Chapter Three

The royal palace guard walked silently with Princess Snow White. Reed had his sword at the ready, just in case, and continuously kept a vigilant eye for anything that might be threatening. He didn't realize, at first, that they were going deeper into the woods instead of along the edge. It was getting late and the prince suitor she was to meet today would be arriving soon. He'd tried to get her to turn back a while ago but she told him to leave her if he wanted, so he remained quiet as they walked, his senses tuned for anything out of the ordinary. However, Reed could no longer remain silent. He knew he had to get her back to the safety of the palace walls. He turned to her and couldn't help but smile as she admired everything she passed, her eyes wide in awe.

During her explorations, Snow had tilted her head, stopping on occasion as she listened to the unique noises the forest provided. She'd lost track of time, enjoying all the new things around her, all the novel sounds, sights and smells. She was perplexed as to why it was considered so dangerous. She'd yet to come upon anything more dangerous than a rabbit or squirrel. Albeit, she was grateful for the serenity, but she couldn't help wondering what everyone had made such a fuss about. Her stuffed lion could've taken care of anything they had come upon thus far.

Snow White still loved her favorite childhood toy. She loved lions, finding them fierce and yet beautiful. When her father had given her the stuffed lion, she carried it with her everywhere. Even to this day, it either sat on her lap as she looked out her bedroom window or she cuddled it as she slept. During the few attempts to sneak into the forest after her nightmares, she carried the toy in front of her, planning on it protecting her should she need to be rescued. She never made it out with the toy lion, but it didn't stop her thinking about her favorite childhood toy.

Upon Reed's insistence, as well as the lateness of the hour and her meeting with the prince of the week, Snow White was about to turn back for home. However, it was then she noticed a clearing and the most darling-looking cottage she had ever beheld. It looked like something one would see in a fairytale and, without hesitation, she ran toward it, startling Reed with her impromptu action.

Reed's stomach dropped as he realized where they were, and if they got back safely it would be a miracle. He tried to stop her, but she was fast and slipped out of his grasp as he went to reach for her. Whispering harshly and praying the inhabitants of the cottage weren't home, he called to her.

"Princess White. *No! No!* Come back. We must escape *now,* before they're aware we're here."

Snow White didn't heed him as she barreled forward to investigate such a quaint structure in the middle of the woods. She heard the royal dragoon pursuing and calling to her, but her curiosity was too great. She needed to peek inside. She promised herself she would behave and return home as soon as she peered into the interior of the little thatched-roof, domed cottage.

The royal guard pursued her, his fear for both of them intensifying. As she'd stopped to gaze into the window of the cabin, Reed caught up to her and pulled her close. At this point, he didn't care if he got hung by his toenails for touching her. He had to protect her. As he spun around with her to drag her back, he realized it was too late. Pushing her behind him with the building at her back, he lifted his sword to the seven little men that suddenly surrounded them.

Hunger burned in their dark, beady, little eyes. Although no more than three-to-four feet tall, they were muscular. Five had long, varying lengths of matted dark hair. One sported short dark hair unevenly cropped in a mop style, and one was bald and clean shaven, making him the exception to the others. All the rest of them had scraggily beards, many with pieces of unspeakable things caught in them or heavily matted from heaven-only-knew what. Their clothes were disheveled, some with holes in the knees or elbows. Soot and grime covered them, some of it heavier on a couple of them. Their grubby hands, holding various instruments of weaponry, were darken with stains from uncleanliness. It was their eyes, though, that drew Snow's attention the most. She'd never seen such hatred in someone's eyes before, especially for someone they didn't know. She was about to put her hand out in a gentle gesture, but stopped when Reed pushed her back farther in a futile attempt to keep her hidden and probably safe. Only then did she realize there were seven of them. Seven little men, who if cleaned and wore pointy hats could look like the adorable little gnomes from her mother's garden, or worse, her month-long nightmares when she was a child. Suddenly, those horrible remnants of her nighttime ordeal as a youth emerged forcefully into her present thoughts and she recoiled back against the building. Maybe her dreams were prophetic but slightly skewed somehow from what was currently occurring.

Reed turned his attention to the one who was more individualistic from the rest. The man was bald and wore glasses and appeared to be the eldest and wisest of the bunch. But then, looks could also be deceiving. Reed took the chance the bald one was the leader of the group, if they even had a leader. He hoped he could talk their way out of this situation, hoped he wouldn't have to fight seven men and could get Princess Snow safely back to the castle and its surrounding walls. Reed quickly realized, however, that it was a wishful thought only. He kept an eye on each of them as best as he could as they slowly moved to encompass them.

The seven men moved in such a way as to form a semicircle around them, their cottage closing the circle. The bald one with glasses took a step forward. He could easily discern the two interlopers were from the palace beyond their woods because of the richness of the clothes the woman wore and the royal emblem on the male brandishing a sword at them.

"You are trespassing."

"We apologize for encroaching upon your land. We will gladly leave immediately and in peace." Reed hoped the men would let them pass, but from the looks of their dirtied, bloodied rags, and the dried blood around their fingertips and mouths, he doubted the princess and he would be so lucky.

"Just because you wear royal garments doesn't give you the right to go wherever you please. Besides, it's extremely rare we have a female in our midst. I don't think some of my brothers have ever even seen a female before now. They will find her curious to see all her curves up close and how they differ from us males."

"I know I have not seen a female before, Doc."

"Neither have I."

"Me either."

"I have and they taste yummy. All soft and tender."

Snow White flinched at the last comment. *Taste? Did he say taste?*

Reed shook his head. *Fuck! They were in the middle of a shit storm without the protection of even an umbrella.* He'd be remembered as the guard who failed his duty and got the only heir to the kingdom eaten by anthropophagites. Growling low, he addressed the one who spoke to them that the other called Doc. "Listen, Doc. If you let us go, I'll make sure you're handsomely rewarded."

Doc shook his head and smiled. His pointed, yellowed fangs almost dripping with saliva. "Thanks for the offer, but I think we'll refuse. Our stomachs would much prefer the meals you provide over the riches you offer. Metal and ore doesn't taste as good as the supple flesh behind you or the meals you yourself will provide."

There is that word again, Snow thought. *Taste.* She feared the word and all it seemed to imply. If others had come to try and rid the forest of these men and were never seen from again, she could only assume they also became part of their meals. Would she and

Reed disappear as well, never to be heard from again? No one finding them? Not even their bones? She had made a horrible mistake and the more she heard from the raggedy, small creatures made her even more certain she should've listened to her family and never ventured here. Her curiosity and stubborn obstinance would get them both killed and it'll solely be her fault.

With Doc's statement, the seven ogre-type men moved in closer, each brandishing a tooled weapon.

Reed snarled at Snow White. "Stay back and out of the way. I'll protect you as best I can."

The princess again contemplated the grave error she'd made by her enthusiasm to see such a quaint structure. Now her bodyguard and friend was about to pay the ultimate price for indulging her whims. She wanted to interfere, but instinctively knew she'd only make matters worse should she try to intercede. Standing as close to the cottage as she could and out of the men's way, she watched nervously as Reed took a step away from her to have some freedom of movement in order to defend Snow White without accidentally harming her.

Doc ran toward Reed brandishing a pair of daggers, which he pulled from a worn leather sheath at his side. Spinning, Reed propelled Doc back with his foot, then lunged for him with his sword. Reed tried to plunge the sword into Doc's chest only to have his movement blocked. The small man caught the sword between his daggers, twisting the sword's blade between his two weapons and thrust back, causing Reed to stumble slightly. Quickly regaining his equilibrium, Reed circled Doc, watching warily. When Doc moved to attack, Reed side-stepped him, kicked his ribs, and swung his sword down executioner style, taking off Doc's head and watching it roll to the side of his body. The ogres seemed surprised that one of their own lay at their feet in a bloody pool, separated into two distinct pieces.

"He killed Doc?"

"He killed Doc!"

"What do we do with Doc now?"

"I think we eat him."

"But it is Doc. He's our brother. Doc is dead?"

"Is Doc dead?"

"I think Doc's dead."

Snow White looked around the men to see the scattered remains of the one known as Doc. She couldn't help but comment under her breath, "I am pretty sure he's dead, unless he can live without a head on his shoulders."

Their anger rose once the shock settled. Their nostrils flared, as some flexed their fingers, while others cracked their knuckles as they circled in an age-old dance that had worked for them for centuries when it came to cornering their prey. As one they moved in towards the royal guardian, totally unconcerned about the female who still hid behind him. Reed looked over his shoulder quickly to make sure Princess Snow White was safe, at least for the moment, and warned her to run if given the chance in a soft growl that he hoped would not be heard by the six ogres that were left and closing the gap between them.

Snow White acknowledged the command despite being worried about the consequences of her bodyguard should he be captured while she was securing her own safety. With the six remaining ogres moving towards Reed, Princess White took the opportunity to run towards the woods. She did not look back, for she knew if she did, they would both be done for. Her best chance was to escape and return with more guards to rescue Reed. She had to get to the safety of her home. A couple of men saw her and took chase while the remaining four stayed to confront the palace guard.

The royal dragoon had been well trained. He wouldn't give them a chance to defeat him or recapture the princess as long as there was breath in his body. Planting his left foot into the ground for stable balance, he thrust his sword back to hit the one trying to flank him. He then pushed forward to attack the ogre closest to him. Spinning the sword with a flick of his wrist, he was able to slice one across the chest, who howled with pain and moved farther out of the way. Reed lunged to his side and pierced the sword into the belly of another ogre moving in for a strike.

Stepping back quickly, the palace bodyguard spun and swung his sword in a wide arc. The previously stabbed being was too slow to duck or move out of the way and his head was also lopped off his shoulders. However, this did not slow down the other three who assaulted him en masse. The ogres pummeled Reed with both weapons and fists. They were able to get the sword away from the royal guard as they continued to smite him down. When Reed finally succumbed to the onslaught, the small creatures dragged him inside and securely tied him up.

The other two creatures gave Snow White a chase through the woods. Problem was, they were highly intimate with the lands, whereas she was very unfamiliar and became easily disoriented. She soon found herself trapped and turned to face the two chasing beings now blocking her escape. She quickly looked around for a weapon and found a good-sized limb nearby. Scooping it up, she brandished it like a sword as she had seen Reed do, trying to keep them away while still looking for an outlet to dash by them and try another escape route. She could only hope to find assistance and thereby save Reed, as well as evade this nightmare she'd found herself a part of.

Swishing the branch around her, the two men laughed at Snow's feeble attempts. They were seasoned cannibals and often had to fight experienced men to attain their meals. This slip of a woman was nowhere near as adept as others they had captured over the past decades, yet they had to admire her foolish endeavors in trying to fend them off. They took up positions and attacked her from either side. While she was able to hold one at bay, the other was able to get behind her and wrap his arms around her, tightly squeezing to prevent her from further attacks. He used his strength, squeezing firmly to get her to drop the branch, then the two of them took the struggling female beauty back to their cottage.

When the four men inside heard the other two returning with a screeching female, they left Reed alone so they could assist in carrying in a struggling she-demon who twisted and clawed at them despite fighting a losing battle.

Snow's clothes were ripped from her as they struggled to subdue her. She had broken the nose of one of her attackers while another hobbled from a swift, unladylike kick to his family jewels in her battle to avoid being tossed into their holding facility. A couple of the grubby little men tried to pull at her clothing or look under it. Some were touching her inappropriately, groping and grabbing at her breasts, thighs or ass as others tried to restrain her. It took all of them to overpower her enough in order to throw her in the cage they had prepared for her and lock it up. Only then could they return their attention to Reed restrained on a long wooden table, which showed red splatter, horrible stains, and shiny bits of viscous matter upon it.

Snow White rattled the cage they imprisoned her in, worry shaking her to her very core.

"Let us go! Let us out of here!"

They had her personal bodyguard strapped to a table and it didn't look like a good place to be. What were they going to do to them? Why were they being held captive? What could the small, grubby men possibly want with them? Did the ogres not realize they were royalty and could afford them anything they desired should they only show mercy and release them unharmed? The short, dirty creatures were unconcerned that she and her guard would be sorely missed. They laughed at her arguments that others would be searching for her and the royal dragoon.

"No one can find us and they have tried for decades. All their attempts have resulted in providing us with more delicious meals. Which, of course, is just what you two will be. We can get several meals from him alone. Your nubile flesh will be like a rich, decadent dessert. A delicacy. My mouth is watering at but the mere thought of how delectable you're going to be."

Chapter Four

Reed tossed his head slightly as he slowly regained consciousness. As he became more aware, he struggled against the ropes that held him immobile on the wooden surface he was bound to. Alertness pressed upon him and he realized Princess Snow White was captured as well. He growled and thrashed more as he fought desperately to be free from the binds that ground him, not only for himself but also to save her. She was his responsibility. She was his obligation to protect and he had failed, miserably.

The five remaining ogres gathered around the guard.

"He killed Doc and Squishy. Do we kill him, too?"

"What do we do with Doc and Squishy?"

"We eat them, too. Waste not, want not."

"We can't do that. Can we?"

"When can we eat him and her? We've never had a her before. I heard about them, but never saw one." The one talking looked towards the cage and grinned, flashing his yellow, jagged fangs.

"Eat him. Play with her, then eat her. I wanna see more of the female. They have bumps in strange places and flat where we aren't. I'm curious."

One of the men waddled towards the cage that held Snow White, appraising her with a sharp eye. After a moment, he spoke, not taking his eyes off of the beautiful woman incarcerated within the wrought-iron cage. "We keep her for later. We salt and cure Doc and Squishy. We eat the guard now. Fresh meat is, after all, the best. Doc and Squishy aren't fresh any longer, so they will work well in getting us through the lean times. However, if in fact these two speak the truth and others will be looking for them, we may have an influx of fresh meat for quite a while." His beady eyes roamed the princess, causing her to back against the far end of the cage, trying to escape his evil gaze. She pulled the tattered remains of clothing around her body as she tried to maintain some semblance of modesty.

The ogre called back to the others as he turned to gaze at them individually while he spoke to each in turn. "Slasher, prepare the knives. Gummy, prepare to remove his armor. Crawler, you and Goopy go bring Doc and Squishy from outside and store them in the cellar.

Be sure to cover them with salt to prevent decay of their juicy parts. I'll deal with the princess here."

"Yes, Brains," they each called back in turn to confirm their assignments and dashed off to complete their missions.

Reed thrashed around harder, trying to break free from his restraints. He needed to get free. *Fuck, I won't be a meal for anything, much less grimy, cannibalistic creatures!* He cursed at them, not caring if the princess could hear him and the vulgarity he used. He was beginning to panic as terror of what they were about to do to him pervaded all his cognizant sensibilities. However, as much as he was fearful for himself at that moment, he was just as concerned for Snow White. He needed to get her free. He was desperate to know she would survive and rule the kingdom as was her destiny. He yearned to protect her as he had throughout all the years he watched her grow from a young babe to a beautiful adult woman. He was angry that she was now locked in a rickety iron cage in a quaint cottage because he cared about her enough to refuse her nothing, even when he knew the potential for her safety could and was compromised.

Brains meandered about the small room, making additional preparations while the others completed his instructions, ignoring the pleading from Snow White and the agitation of the royal guard as he tried to break free from the secured bonds around him. After a while, even she was getting on his nerves. "Will you be quiet, already? Or at least scream and howl? I actually find that enjoyable, like music to my pointed ears. Your incessant nagging is a bit obnoxious and irritating. Shut up or I'll cut your tongue out and eat it before your eyes."

Brains moved closer to the cage as he tilted his head. "You know, I might just do that anyways."

She clammed up momentarily, although she moved closer, gripping the metal as she looked down at her tormentor. "I'll see you all dead before you have the chance."

"Big words from someone who is behind bars and our prisoner." Brains spun away as Doc and Squishy were brought in by Crawler and Goopy. He led them to the back.

While they were alone, Reed turned to his ward. "Princess, please take advantage of any opportunity to escape. Your safety is of the utmost importance. I'm sorry I didn't succeed in protecting you better. I should never have let you talk me into putting your safety at risk. I deserve my fate for my recklessness. You don't."

"No, Reed. No. It's most certainly my fault and I take full responsibility. I should've listened to your warnings. I shouldn't have been so curious. For my inquisitiveness, you're going to end up suffering, paying the ultimate price for my obstinate tendencies. Surely the beasts were incorrect? Others will come for us. Others will find us. Others will *save* us. We just have to hold on."

Reed laid still for a moment, gazing at Snow White. Even in a tattered-clothed state, dirty from the skirmish with the ogres who chased her down and captured her, she was still beautiful. He didn't have the heart to tell her the ogres were right. They wouldn't be found, just as all those who had tried in the past to find this cottage had never returned.

"Let's just get out of here and we can worry about who is to blame later." He didn't want her to lose her hope, even if it was misplaced.

Renewing his battle with the ties that bound him, Reed desperately tried to get free. His efforts increased as the ogres returned to the room, gathering around his incapacitated form while they brandished rusty, blood-stained, worn knives. Snow White cried out, trying to reach for him as they blocked her view with their own bodies. They may have hidden what they did to him from her vantage point, but they could not block the sound that pierced the air as Reed's screams of pure torment were torn from his throat.

Chapter Five

Prince Donnigan rode deeper into the forest. He had a vague idea of where to go. He was following the path that was indicated to him from beneath Princess Snow White's window that originally enticed her to such a foolhardy excursion. When the trail became too convoluted to determine which way he should continue, he dismounted his steed and squatted to the ground. He used all of his tracking abilities, trying to gain some indication of the direction Snow White and her companion might have traversed. He soon realized he needed better senses then his human ones.

He pushed his long, blond hair back from his intensely rich, blue eyes as he listened to the sounds of the forest, trying to glean its secrets. He stood and turned towards his mount, patting the long mane of the ebony beast.

"Stay alert, my friend. I may have need of you soon."

Donnigan wrapped the reins around the embroidered saddle horn. He watched the equine move off to nibble at some grass while waiting for when she would next be required. He admired his horse, in some cases more than people. No matter what, she was always there for him and he appreciated that more than anything. Not that he didn't like the people of his kingdom, but he preferred his solitude in some cases, and for a very good reason. Although he was a prince, he also had a special trait that very few knew, and those who did, feared. There were many who insisted he marry, gain an heir, but he worried what any future mate might think of his real countenance. The only reason he had come to this land was because he had heard of the love and kindness of Princess Snow White. From the stories that have spread across the lands, he believed he might stand a chance in winning her hand and thereby saving his kingdom. Only a true gentle spirit could accept what he could become. He had so much to offer the one who cared for him, who wasn't afraid of who or what he was and who would stand by him regardless of his heritage. However, he also had to trust someone with the very essence of his soul before he could offer his heart. Would Snow White be the woman he could surrender himself to completely? Would she be the one who would love him unconditionally? Or would she turn out to be a disappointment as all the others have been? Regardless of the outcome of their meeting, he had to find her, or his musing would prove for naught.

Needless to say he was surprised when he learned of her disappearance. At first Prince Donnigan was sure she had learned the truth of him somehow and disappeared to avoid the meeting. However, with King Nicholas' elucidations of the situation, he realized she knew nothing of his condition. According to the king, she didn't even know of the dangers that lay beyond the walls of her own palace grounds. Maybe with Snow White, he'd have a chance to be accepted for what he was. That thought continuously wormed its way through his soul with almost every breath he took. He needed to stop the thought and deal with the reality of the current dilemma. She might be the one, she might not; but with her gone, he'd never know either way. Of course he had to find her, which he was not apt to do within his current physical limitations.

He removed a few vestiges of clothing and shoved them in the saddlebag. Removing a thin undergarment from the bag, he put it on the ground. He had to smirk at the memory of the look King Nicholas bestowed upon him at his request for something that the princess wore recently and contained her scent. If only he knew the truth, Nicholas would have been astounded and might have even refused him. Thankfully, the king was far more interested in getting his daughter back that he didn't concern himself with specifics and immediately had an article of cloth brought to Prince Donnigan.

Stepping away from his mare, he willed himself to change. His already long, blond hair grew and became fuller. His blue eyes turned amber. His teeth elongated into fangs while his fingers gnarled into claws as tawny fur covered his entire body. Falling onto all fours, he gave out a loud roar that shook the trees and caused a cloud of dust to swirl around him. He knew the sound of his kingly bellow could be heard for miles. The sound would warn those who dared harm royalty that he was coming.

Although only a prince, Donnigan was king of the jungle in this form. Putting his nose to Snow White's garment, he breathed in her scent. Opening his jaws, he allowed his olfactory organ on the roof of his mouth to intake the unique odor that was the woman of whom he sought. Leaving the cloth on the ground, he moved away on all fours. His nose pressed to the ground, then the air. He searched using his lion senses. In this form, Prince Donnigan could hear the shrieks of a man in intense agony. Better yet, the smell of Princess Snow White laid in the same direction as the cacophony that rent throughout the woods. He estimated they were a little less than a mile away and took off in a burst of speed towards them. Donnigan would be able to approach their location silently as a result of the soft pads of his species, which made his movements stealthy. He also knew his steed would follow as she was trained to do.

Chapter Six

Snow White wept softly in the corner of the cage. The screams from Reed were ear piercing. They may have been slicing Reed, but his cries cut her to her very core. This was her fault. Her faithful friend and guardian was being tortured and she could do nothing to stop it, no matter how much she wanted to. Give her one brief moment with a weapon and she would be his revenge. Alas, she was just as trapped as Reed was, and just as useless. The mere thought tortured her deeply. She wished she could turn back time, wished she had listened to her parents and Reed, wished her curiosity hadn't gotten the better of her and, most of all, she wished she could do *anything* to help him.

Why had she been so selfish wanting to experience the forest beyond her window for so many years? Why had her parents and the others kept her in such a protective bubble as to safeguard her and keep her uninformed about what horrors actually lay beyond the gilded gates of her home? Did they think she couldn't handle the truth of the abominations that occurred in their realm? Were they timorous not being able to prevent the existence of such atrocities from occurring?

Or embarrassed to have not succeeded in making and keeping their lands safe from such monstrosities? Nothing else made sense to her. She couldn't believe that people who loved her as much as her parents did would purposely hide the dangerous anathemas of their kingdom, except to shield her from such heinous barbarities. Had she known, even a minute inkling of what the beautiful greenery shielded, she'd never have come and exposed Reed to such danger.

She didn't worry about herself as much as she did those in her kingdom. It bothered her greatly that her people have been plagued by fears of the area and these creatures, especially the man who, in effect, helped raise her. Reed had been by her side for as long as she could remember, assigned to make sure she was safe from all the evils that might befall her, even if it was of her own doing. It was Reed that picked her up when she fell off her horse as a child while learning how to ride. It was Reed who would scoop her up and carry her when she was too tired to walk. And it was Reed who kept others away while she sat under the apple tree reading in her need to hide from all the others who fawned over her to the point she was uncomfortable.

Reed seemed to understand her desire to avoid everyone for a few hours, to find some peace for herself and shirk her princess duties. There were times she didn't read, but sat and daydreamed, and there were other days when she would ask Reed to join her and they would discuss a multitude of various subjects. Reed was the one who aided her knowledge of what went on in the kingdom so she was prepared to help those she would meet later on. In truth, she obtained her reputation for kindness and understanding because of her dialogue with the royal dragoon. She learned just as much from him as she did her own tutors, but it wasn't reading and writing, history or math Reed taught her, but how to handle the issues and concerns of the people who resided in her kingdom. She didn't know what she would've done without him, and now, because of her, he was suffering immensely.

The cannibalistic ogres spent hours cutting, slicing, and enjoying their meal with gusto, which unfortunately was the struggling, alive body of the royal dragoon. They'd barely spoken during their meal, only to ask for the passing of something out of their reach or to mention how tasty he was. Those comments all but made her vomit as she gagged and tried to keep her own bile down. Surely there was some way to get out of here, some way to rescue her guardian and save them both. *This was a nightmare! It had to be!* Yet, as the minutes turned into hours, hope within her began to diminish and despair took over.

At one point, she thought she was so despondent that she was beginning to hallucinate. She would've sworn over all the shrieking and bellowing she heard a lion's roar. Her kingdom didn't have lions, that she was aware of. Even so, it would do nothing to help her or her predicament even if the wooded forest contained such a species. All it did was give her an additional fear that if she did manage by some miracle to escape, then she'd have to worry about a pride of lions roaming the area. Most likely they'd smell the blood of her guardian, which would do nothing more than attract the carnivorous animals to them. She knew she wasn't strong or powerful enough to even contemplate fighting off a lion, especially when she couldn't even figure out how to gain her freedom and rescue her bodyguard.

Albeit, there was a momentary foolish notion the lion in her dream all those years ago, or even her stuffed lion, somehow came to life and was going to rescue and protect her. She knew she was being foolish, but she couldn't help the wayward idea. She didn't need to be hoping for some ridiculous, optimistic speculation that was only her imagination. She had to look for viable ways to escape, and keeping her head in the clouds wasn't going to achieve such an unobtainable goal at this time.

Although the cacophony from Reed's cries was finally silenced as he blissfully passed out, the slurping and munching sounds continued. Those were just as bad, if not worse, to Snow White's ears. She wished for something to make her faint as well, so she'd no longer have to listen to the resonance of the creatures gnawing and noisily masticating on her lifelong companion.

Princess Snow White jumped, hitting her arm on the bar cage, when the front door of the cottage crashed flat against the floor. Amazed, she gawked at the huge lion that literally took up the entire frame of the small abode. At first she thought it might be her wishful imagination, but even the ogres stopped and looked askew at the interruption. Terror flashed across their bloodied faces. The five cannibal ogres scattered every which way, two even running into each other and knocking the other down in their haste. If circumstances were different, Snow might have considered the whole thing comical.

Snow White wondered if there was hope in surviving this ordeal. She assumed the lion had been attracted to the smell of blood—blood the men caused by delving into the flesh of the royal dragoon. Reed was still lying on the table, unconscious and unaware of the current threat, while she was locked in an iron cage, unable to do anything but be an unwilling observer.

The lion stood still. He looked around as if looking for something in particular and Snow feared it would be Reed, the blood having attracted him. But after a few moments, the majestic creature moved towards her cage and she cringed, even though she was safely behind the bars. His head turned again as if to take in the current situation before he pounced upon the closest ogre, Goopy. The lion literally broke Goopy's back between the heaviness and the power behind the leap, then his claws tore it open in one swipe, severing the spinal cord. The king of beasts then turned towards

Crawler, his sharp paw lacerating the anthropophagite in a single stroke. Without hesitation, the lion swiveled and pounced on Gummy. He took a massive bite from the small man's throat, immediately crushing his windpipe, and left him gurgling in his final death throes. Brains and Slasher managed to dash outside while their compatriots were being slaughtered by the lion. The lion's mane was drenched in blood. He didn't seem too worried about the two small men temporarily evading his execution. He probably would get them soon enough. Looking around quickly, he headed towards the cage again and she wondered why he kept approaching it when others were more readily available, including Reed. She was surprised when he used his powerful strength in his forepaws and pushed against the bars, letting the door rip from its hinges.

Snow was petrified at the huge beast. She had assumed she was safe within the cage, yet he broke through the bars as easily as if they were made of straw. She backed against the furthest barrier from the door as it crashed inward. She stood still, paralyzed with her fear of him, sure he could smell her terror. She had just watched him easily manhandle and kill three of her captors as efficiently and quickly as if they were made of nothing more than grapes under his feet instead of strong, able-bodied men.

Without any further glance at Snow White, he backed up and headed out of the cottage in order to pursue the last two dwarf anthropophagites. She was stunned as she watched the king of beasts leave, and surprised he didn't go after her or Reed. After a few split seconds of hesitation, she broke free of her stupor. There was no time to dally, for she didn't know when any of them might return. Bursting out of the now-opened containment area to the table, she snatched Reed's sword from the back wall.

She kept the sword by her side as she bent over Reed. He was barely still alive. Being this close, she could see all the damage they had done to him. Skin peeled away, sinew chopped out and missing. His foot had been removed. The fact he was alert for most of this torture amazed yet sickened her enormously. She literally turned away for a moment to let the bile settle back down from viewing all the destruction his body endured. She could hear the screams and cries sharply cut off with gurgling sounds from beyond the cottage entrance. Minutes ticked by as the stillness of the woods became almost deafening. Sensing more than seeing, Snow White lifted the sword and faced the doorway as the large lion returned to stand within its small frame. She would defend her wounded friend and herself if need be, though something about this beast made her hesitate from a full onslaught attack. Maybe because he released her from her prison, as if knowing not to harm her. She waited and watched to see if he would attack her as he had the dreadful ogres.

Chapter Seven

Donnigan gazed at the princess, who stood ready to fight. All he had heard about her was true. She was extremely beautiful, her torn garments doing little to hide her feminine attributes. Her beauty called to his lion. He wanted to claim her and make her his. Feel that soft subtle flesh under his hands as he kissed and licked every inch of her body. He desired to feel the hot, wetness sheath his hard member as he made love to her over and over again until she screamed his name begging for him to stop. He shook his mane to get such lecherous thoughts out of his mind.

However, he was surprised she appeared more concerned in protecting the injured man on the table than hiding her modesty. He didn't mean to, but couldn't help but instantly compare her to so many others he had met over the years. Where they would not have cared less for someone they would consider beneath them, Snow was willing to protect her guard with her very life. She brandished the sword, although not expertly, with a definitive knowledge and command at her control. He was well aware that she would defend both her guard and herself to the death against him, should the need arise. Had he not been interested in her previously, he would be now. This determined young woman enticed him as none had ever before. He wanted her as his wife, to rule by his side. She was everything he could want in a woman. Beauty, courage, a kick-ass body, and spunk. His fear was she would spurn him for what he was. He could only pray she would come to him on her own, love him for what he was inside. He realized he best get the shock over with and see if he stood a chance at being her swain. It wasn't an easy choice, and he had to admit it was easier to fight in a battle than it was to shift into a man in front of her. She was what he wanted. From the moment he saw her in the cage, he knew it. Again, thoughts of her naked and writhing beneath him flashed in his mind and he knew he'd have to be upfront with her from the start. He wanted to be accepted by her and he felt he might stand a chance, but if she didn't trust him, or his abilities scared her, he'd have no hope left in finding a mate for himself. He realized the second he beheld her in person and his lion roared within that he'd never desire another. Whether or not she accepted him, his lion had claimed her as his and no one else would suffice. He had to be truthful to her. After several moments, he decided to take the only chance he had and risk everything.

As they stared at each other, his amber eyes turned blue. The bloodied mane became shorter. His elongated fangs reduced as his face scrunched back into a human visage. Before her very eyes, he changed from a lion into a man crouched on the floor. Gauging her reaction, he stood up slowly and reached for a towel lying nearby to dip in water and wash his face, turning his back to her and the sword she wielded.

"I won't harm you. I'm here to save you and return you to your father."

Snow's eyes widened. To see the lion change to that of a man was something she'd never believe possible before. She couldn't help but take in every part of him. Not only was he a man, he was a very striking man *and* he was nude. She'd never seen a man nude before and her eyes were immediately attracted to his penis which stood slightly erect and twitching. *Why did it do that? Was that normal?* When he used the towel to cover his member, she forced herself to focus on the matter at hand.

"Who are you? Not that I'm ungrateful for your assistance, for I am, but I'm also curious."

He turned around to face her. "You're not frightened of me? Of what I am? What I just was?"

"I don't understand it and I probably should be terrified out of my wits, but...I'm not. So, will you tell me who you are?" She couldn't explain to herself why she was so calm and comfortable with him, there was no way she'd be able to elucidate.

Donnigan chuckled softly. "My name is Prince Donnigan. I'm from the kingdom of Panthera. We were scheduled to meet today, although I do believe under more illustrious conditions than a cottage in the middle of the woods owned by a group of dwarf man-eaters and me covered in their blood." He sighed softly and ran a hand through his long hair. "Listen. I know you're unsure of what I am, of what I can become, but I'd prefer you keep it our secret in return for saving your lives. Many folks are not ready to handle someone like me if they knew. I'll not ask to become an official suitor if you don't desire it. However, I also realize two things.

One, a lot has happened and you're probably in a bit of shock, and two, your guard is going to bleed to death if we don't get him help as soon as possible. My steed is outside and can get you both back quickly and safely after I cauterize the wound. Otherwise he'll bleed out before we can get him aid."

The princess slowly lowered the sword as Donnigan spoke. He made a good deal of rational sense, and he was also correct in realizing that Reed needed care if he were to survive at all. Surprisingly, Donnigan didn't scare her. If anything, she was intrigued by him and his special gift. He saved her and exposed himself to her when he didn't have to do either.

He realized she was also aware of this. Oddly, the fact she accepted him so easily made him worry. Could anyone be as accepting as she was? Donnigan wasn't sure, but maybe it was because she was still in shock, or maybe she feared she would never see her family and friends again and this spurred her acceptability more readily. He could only hope she was as genuine as she appeared. He didn't think he would be able to handle the disappointment should she suddenly change her mind and reject him. True, no one liked to be spurned, but he had opened himself up to her, bared his secret and his soul in order to protect her and, as a result, hoped beyond hope she wouldn't take his heart and stomp on it before she left him cringing in the dust, for she had the ability to do that. Suddenly, he had to wonder what had happened that someone he just met could have that power over him, to destroy his entire soul if she desired. Yes, she was beauty beyond reproach, but it was more than that. Her beauty touched her soul and shone so brightly he knew no one could resist her charms. Including him. He realized it might also be because he shared with her something he had never shared with another. She had seen what he really was, knew the dangerous beast who lived just below the surface and sometimes clawed to get out and have the freedom to do as he pleased. Albeit, it usually didn't involve killing so many. His beast didn't mind. He wanted—no, needed—to save her, and he took a huge chance in immediately showing her the most intimate part of him.

Donnigan busied himself with preparing a hot iron in order to still the flow of the lost limb. As he stood over Reed for the first time, even he was sickened by what the cannibals had done to one such as the royal dragoon. To attain such a position, he knew, the man was well-trained, and his duties meant he was probably one of the best within the palace, yet the dwarves managed to make mince-meat of him and it sickened the prince greatly. Donnigan could only imagine what Snow went through as she watched what they did to such a strong man.

When the iron was hot, he asked Snow to hold his shoulders and her breath. The smell of burning flesh was horrible and Donnigan was also sure the man would momentarily awaken from the pain before he would pass out again.

As Snow White turned her head and held her breath after a big gulp of air, he pressed the hot iron against the wound. Once the wound was cauterized, Donnigan took some additional towels and wrapped the appendage. As he moved to lift Reed off the table, she stilled him with a gentle touch on his arm.

"Thank you for rescuing us. For helping him. I'm deeply indebted to you. And I will keep my promise. I won't tell anyone about your abilities."

"No thanks needed. Saving damsels in distress is a nice change of pace from the everyday grind of preparing to rule a kingdom." He started to turn back when she caught his jaw and forced him to look back at her. She stood on her tiptoes and pressed her soft, rosy lips against his before retreating a step back. She was aware of how forward such an action was, but she couldn't help himself. He'd made her feel things she'd never experienced before, including a hot flush to her skin, a warm wetness between her thighs and her stomach doing flips. She just had to know what it would be like to kiss him.

"Should you wish, I'd be honored to have you court me. Your secret will be safe with me, regardless."

Prince Donnigan paused, turning fully back to her. "Are you serious?" He could barely believe it. He wanted her, but after all her recent trials he wasn't about to even push to date her, despite his deepest desire to claim her for his very own. He may be an alpha lion, but knowing what she just endured, he wouldn't force her into anything she was uncomfortable with. Could he be dreaming? Was she really serious? He stared down at her in disbelief, not even positive he heard her correctly yet wishing upon everything that he did.

Princess Snow White smiled softly. "Yes. I am rarely frivolous. Adventurous, stubborn, determined; but rarely frivolous."

He pulled her toward him, kissing her deeply. From the moment he saw her, he could not resist her. He pulled her close, mindless of the stench and dead bodies that surrounded them, or the fact he was still mostly naked, wearing nothing but a towel that was becoming tented. His tongue battered against her lips until she opened them, accepting his exploring tongue within her mouth. After several long moments, they each pulled back. He knew this was neither the time nor place to continue. Despite her willingness to accept him and his advances, they really needed to get to know each other better. But her telling him she wanted the opportunity to do so enthralled him. He knew they would have all the time they needed. "Ready?"

She nodded. "Yes."

Donnigan wrapped up Reed in a couple of the cleanest sheets he could find and carried him to the horse that was waiting outside. Setting Reed down,

Donnigan went to his saddlebag and removed the articles of clothing he had placed there earlier. Handing them to Snow White so that she could cover herself appropriately, he tended Reed as best as he could. When the princess was once again demur, he lifted Snow White onto the steed. Cautiously, he then lifted Reed to be cradled by her. Taking the reins, he jogged back towards the princess' castle.

Chapter Eight

As they walked slowly back towards the palace, Donnigan and Snow had a chance to talk. With everything Reed had just been through, Donnigan didn't want the horse to jostle him any more than necessary. Although they cauterized the wound and wrapped it as best they could, Donnigan knew it was a tricky situation. They had to hurry to get him proper medical attention, but they also couldn't be too quick as to reopen the injury and have him bleed out in the process.

At first, the two were quiet as they made their way through the wooded area. Snow was constantly checking on Reed and Donnigan admired the attention she gave to her friend. Finally, he couldn't resist asking her a couple of questions as he broke the tranquil quiet. "Why did you run away? Were you that frightened to meet me?"

Snow gasped softly. "No. It wasn't that at all. I didn't run away. I wanted to explore."

"So this is the time, when we were to meet, you chose to explore the woods? Against your father's wishes?"

"Not exactly. I'd wanted to come for a number of years, but obeyed my father. With everything he had gone through with my step-mother, and her trying to poison us both, I didn't wish to be a burden to him, but there was this sense of urgency in me this morning. The thought that once I met you, that would be it and I'd never have another chance again. I just had to take the opportunity while it still existed."

"What happened to your mother? What happened with your step-mother? I mean, if you don't mind my asking."

"It's okay. My mother died from an illness when I was very young. My father, in his grief, remarried to ensure I'd have a female figure to look up to, but she wanted the kingdom for herself, and as a result, tried to feed us apples filled with poison. Our servants are allowed to take fruit if they wish and one of them took one of the apples. She died almost immediately. It was only then we realized they were all poisoned. My father ousted her immediately when she admitted it was her behind such a horrendous and treacherous act. I never wanted to do something to make him worry about me.

"This morning, though, I felt it was imperative to go. I can't explain it."

"I can understand the need to give into your compulsions. Have you always wanted to go exploring? Or was this a recent idea?" Donnigan was trying to understand why she hadn't tried to venture into the woods earlier. He still had the sneaking suspicion she ran away so she wouldn't have to meet him. Did she, in fact, know what he was beforehand? Is that why she wasn't scared of him when she saw him shift? Nothing else made sense to him, but he also detested the fact he wasn't trusting of her so readily. She had given him no clear reason to be so skeptical of her. Maybe it was because all the others he had met before were of dubious character. He didn't want to believe that with Snow White, but he honestly just didn't know what to think.

Snow checked on Reed once again to make sure he was still out but okay. "No. It's not a recent idea, but it is a recent attempt. When I was younger, I wanted to go in the forest all the time. I hated it was forbidden to me and I never understood why. When I was about ten, my father read me Aesop's fable of *Androcles and the Lion*.

I don't know why, but it had a very strong effect on me. Every night after, I dreamt of a lion being abused by seven creatures, chained and tortured. In some of my dreams, I was able to help him, but the creatures got me. In others, I failed entirely. I usually ended up running away to escape the wrath of the cruel men. The nightmares lasted for weeks and I barely got any sleep. I remember how ill I became, how tired and listless. About a month or so later, my father brought me a stuffed toy lion. Where he found it, I'll probably never know, but once he gave it to me, I slept for the first time in weeks. Somehow, this lion calmed me, protecting me from my nightmares. I know it's silly, but it's how I felt. I still sleep with that lion every night. Lions have become my favorite animal and I have a very soft heart for them.

"I'd never seen a real one until you burst through that door. And, as in my dreams, he, I mean you, saved me from the nightmare I was enduring. Only reality is even better, for it comes with a man attached to the lion, and one who's brave and strong. Without even knowing me, you forged ahead to bring me and Reed back home safely and rid our woods from such despicable creatures.

"I know this sounds impossible, but I think—no, I believe—you came to protect me now just as your spirit protected me all those years ago. I'm not afraid of you because a part of me has always known you'd come. A part of me has always loved you. I've just been waiting all this time, and I just didn't know what I was waiting for until you burst down that door."

As she spoke, he couldn't help but look back up at her. This couldn't possibly be real! What she was saying, her words, the emotions behind them, the truth, it was mind boggling to him. Maybe she was right and they were supposed to meet. Maybe in her feeling that sense of urgency to explore, today of all days, was the catalyst to push him to seek her out and unwittingly reveal himself as early as he had. Would he have been as interested in her, as enthralled, if events hadn't played out the way they had and he had met the princess in her palace under the auspices of her father and chaperones?

He was startled out of his reverie when she softly asked him something. It took a moment for the words to actually register. He realized she had asked about his unique gifts. Gifts. There were times he thought of them more as a curse than an actual gift.

"I'm not that unique of a man, gifted with the ability to change forms into a lion. This gift, as you call it, was inherited from my mother's lineage as a gift from the gods. Only the males of her line inherit the trait to change forms at will, giving us increased stamina, veracity, power, and strength. The ability also bestowed upon us the inherent attributes of lions, such as their sense of smell, hearing, and stealthy movements." Donnigan went on to explain he was the eldest of five siblings and had been pressured to find a wife. He hadn't ever thought to find someone like Snow and he couldn't be more grateful.

The more he told her, confided in her, the more she fell in love with him. The palace walls loomed ahead. A more welcoming sight Princess Snow White couldn't remember. The palace guards saw their approach and alerted the king of their impending arrival. The carriage paths were quickly lined with servants and guards. When a sweaty Donnigan drew up in front of the palace steps where King Nicholas awaited them, he immediately asked for the royal physician to be brought for Reed.

During the ride, Reed regained consciousness momentarily every now and again, but was willing to relax as he became aware they were free of their torturous captors and headed back to the castle. Reed listened to their conversation only long enough to ascertain Donnigan wasn't a threat. Only then did he allow himself to succumb back into oblivion. Servant hands lifted Reed from Snow White's grasp and carried him inside to be attended by the palace doctor. Prince Donnigan moved to help Snow White off his steed and he kept his arm around her waist.

"As promised, my liege, I have returned your daughter safely home. But I also told you that my price would be extreme."

King Nicholas peered at the smug prince. The younger man stood with his chin jutted out, a smirk evident on his countenance as his posture radiated authority. Originally he had planned on demanding something else for his payment, but at Snow White's assured willingness, he readily accepted her offer to be his wife. After a few moments, Donnigan lowered his arm from the princess' waist and moved forward a few steps. Keeping his head high, he lowered his voice to the king.

"My payment is your daughter's hand in marriage."

The king was about to protest but hesitated when Snow White stepped beside Donnigan and slipped her hand into his. "I agree to his payment request, Father. I have chosen him to be my sovereign and my husband."

Nicholas glanced between the two of them. After hedging a bit longer, he smiled and looked up at the crowd to address them. "My daughter, Snow White, is to be married to Prince Donnigan of Panthera. May they live long and rule with a loving hand the two kingdoms that will be merged as a result of their union."

Cheers rang throughout the palace grounds.

Chapter Nine

Six Months Later

The wedding day had finally arrived. Snow White stood in front of the mirror. Normally, it would be only her father giving her away on this day, but she had made a special request. King Nicholas would be on one side of her, and on the other would be the royal dragoon, Reed. He had been forced to retire due to the injuries he had suffered as a result of the dwarf cannibals. He was still weak and healing slowly, but his progress as a whole was amazing, even to the royal physician.

A maid called to her that it was time. Snow White directed her steps to the chapel located within the palace garden. Arriving at the stone building, Snow White hugged and kissed her father, then repeated the process with Reed before gently taking his arm with one hand and King Nicholas' arm with the other. She walked slowly down the aisle. She saw little else but the handsome man waiting for her at the altar, a man who saved her and her bodyguard and saw them safely back home. A prince she would spend the rest of her life with, and a lion that she would be enamored with forever.

Epilogue

Princess Snow White ran among the trees of the forest. Her heart beat wildly as she looked over her shoulder to see how close he was as she tried to evade him. She couldn't let him find her. Turning a bend in the pathway, she ran into him and screamed. A wall of muscle and height, an immovable force when he chose, she fell onto her ass. The large lion shifted into human form. Roaring out with laughter, Prince Donnigan reached down and helped her to stand. Moving closer to her, he nibbled her neck as he whispered into her ear. "I'll always find you, wife, for you're my soul mate and my love. You'll always be safe and never able to hide from me."

Bending slightly, he placed his arm under the crook of her legs to scoop her up in his arms. Carrying her back to their isolated picnic spot, he set her down on the blanket gently. He continued to look deeply into her eyes as his hands slowly removed her clothing, leaving her bare to his touch and sight. "You're the most beautiful woman I've ever laid eyes on. I'm forever thankful you're mine."

Although a bit shy yet, she let her hands roam over his naked body. He almost laughed at how shaky her hands still were after being together the past couple of weeks. He kissed her neck and shoulders the entire time he worked at stripping her as bare as the day she was born.

Snow White pulled him to her, rolling him over. She straddled him as her hands caressed his torso, just admiring him. "Mine," she groaned before she captured his lips again.

Donnigan slid his hands down her back and over her bottom, giving it a firm squeeze as they kissed. "Mine at last."

"Now that we've that cleared up," she teased him, moving to kiss and lick his neck, her hands on his body. She caressed and rubbed against him, feeling him get hard beneath her touch.

Donnigan moaned softly against her lips as he held her close, happy that she was now his wife. He was even happier that she truly loved him. He took his time to slide his hands over her curves, wanting to make love to her slowly.

She licked her way down his chest, playing with first one nipple and then the other, slowly torturing both. By not giving him access to her body, despite how much her sheath ached to have his hardness within her, she continued to prolong their desire.

Donnigan growled low within his chest, enduring the delicious torment at her hands. "Gods, you're amazing."

She clasped his hand with hers and slid him inside of her, gasping at how good he felt within her body. "Donnigan," she moaned and started to slowly move her body against him.

He continued to kiss along the side of her neck as he felt her wet heat surround him. Intertwining the fingers of their clasped hands, he held her tight with his free arm as their tongues dueled. She started to move faster against him, his thrusts matching her rhythm.

The pressure built with their movement. She could feel the sweat from their exertions glisten against her warm skin. Her orgasm built and she swore she saw stars when her body exploded with release. His mouth clamped against hers the moment his hot seed jetted from him. As he kissed her passionately, he left her breathless. She collapsed on top of him.

"My husband. For today and always. I love you so much." Still keeping him inside her, she nuzzled his neck.

Donnigan smiled at her words as he rolled her underneath him, placing soft kisses over her face and neck. "As you are mine from this moment on until infinity, Snow White. I love you with all my heart and soul."

She smiled as she wrapped her legs and arms around him, holding him tight. She needed and loved him more than she ever thought possible. "Forever, Prince Donnigan."

"Forever, Princess Snow White."

She truly had a lion to protect her now.

And they lived happily ever after.

ABOUT THE AUTHOR

Ms. Hawks has always been interested in writing in some form or other. A few years back, she was involved with and then ran a Star Trek Interactive Writing Group which was successful for a number of years. Yes, she is a trekker and proud of it.

A few years back, she received her Master's Degree in Ancient Civilizations, Native American History and United States History.

It was at this time she got involved in role playing on FaceBook, which gave her ample opportunities to grow and hone her writing ability.

She lives in the suburbs of Chicago with her three companions, all males... cats. She travels as much as she can to various Author/Reader conventions and loves to meet established fans and make new ones, some of which she considers friends more than fans. Check out her FB page or website
Laura-Hawks.com

More From Laura Hawks
The Demon Trilogy

Spirit Walker's Saga

Spirit Walker's Saga

Civil War Paranormal

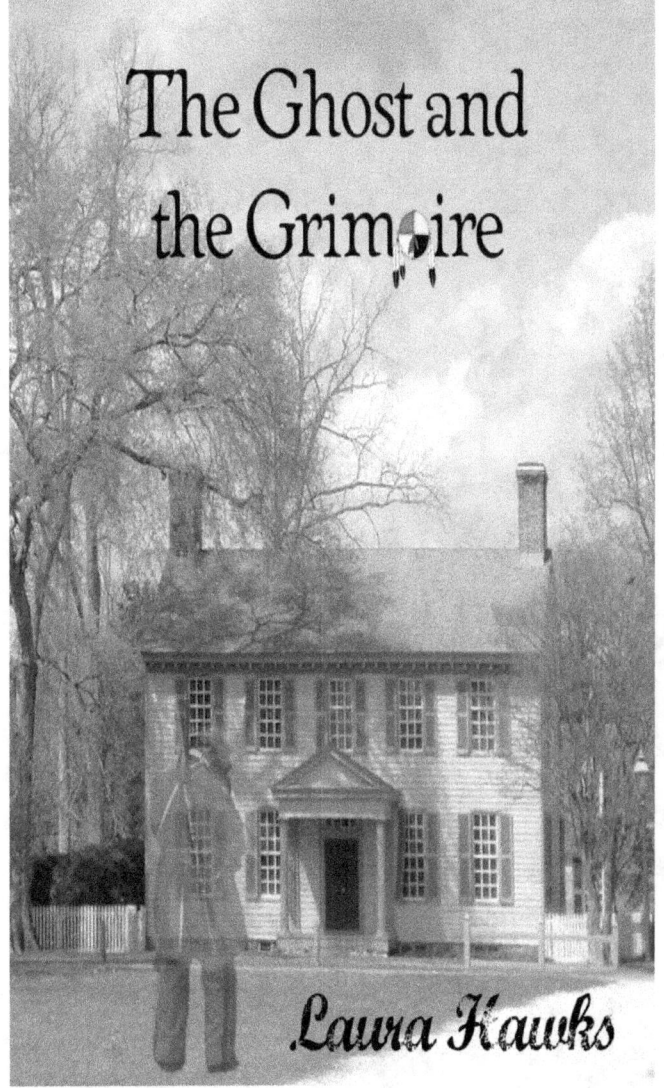

Contemporary Suspense